Sophie Washington
Queen of the Bee

Written by
Tonya Duncan Ellis

Books By
Tonya Duncan Ellis

Sophie Washington: Queen of the Bee

Sophie Washington: The Snitch

Sophie Washington:
Things You Didn't Know About Sophie

Sophie Washington: The Gamer

Sophie Washington: Hurricane

Table of Contents

Chapter 1

Three Little Pigs

In fairy tales, everyone's wish comes true. Jack gets the goose that lays the golden egg. Cinderella finds Prince Charming. Pinocchio becomes a real boy.

My happily ever after is much simpler. I want a pet goldfish. I don't think that's too much to ask.

But my parents do. For the past year they have been putting me off every time I beg them for a pet.

"I'm allergic to cats and dogs," says Mom. "There's no way we could keep a furry animal in the house."

"Well, what about a fish?" I ask.

"I don't know if you're responsible enough to take care of a goldfish, Sophie," says Dad. "You might drop the bowl and get water all over the place."

For a ten-year-old I am *very* responsible. If you forget about the time my brother, Cole, and I had a water fight with the sprinkler in the garage, or when I tied Cole up to a tree to keep him from tagging along with me and my friend Chloe, I'm a model child. I get good grades in school. I'm nice to my friends. And I help out in the house when Mom and Dad ask me to.

Today, I'm making my dream come true! I'm going to convince Dad to let me get a pet goldfish.

I march toward the kitchen in my pink and white polka-dot pajamas and lime green fuzzy slippers. After glancing in the hallway mirror, I push down my two, thick black braids, which stick out on each side of my head like handlebars.

"Good morning," I say to my mother, who is busy in the kitchen making my favorite breakfast of bacon, eggs, grits and homemade pancakes. Since Dad is not up to hear me beg for a fish again, I make my way to the family room to watch a recording of a television show I taped during the school week.

Cole rushes into the room before me and grabs the remote control from the end table before I can reach it.

"Get back!" I yell.

He turns on "Video Rangers", his favorite TV show. Then he puts the remote control under a pillow, sits on it and passes gas.

"Eeeewww! Give me that remote, Cole!" I shriek. "You knew I was getting ready to use it."

"Moooom! I was here first, and now she wants to change the channel," he whines.

"Turn the television off, and you two go get the newspaper and pull the garbage can up to the garage," says Mom, shaking her head and pouring more pancake batter into the skillet. "All this arguing is going to make me burn breakfast."

I clench my fists to keep from wringing Cole's neck.

"Did you tell Mom about the contest?" he loudly yells over blips and bleeps. He is playing a Video Rangers cartridge on his handheld video game now that the television is off.

"What contest?" asks Dad, entering the kitchen.

"Oh, it's nothing really," I say. "Just something Mrs. Green was talking about at school on Friday…"

"It's the big spelling bee, and they want all the kids in the third grade and up to be in it," pipes up Cole. "Mrs. Green said she hopes Sophie signs up, since she's such a great speller."

"That sounds like a wonderful opportunity for you, Sophie," Mom says. "You *are* really good at spelling."

"Sign up first thing Monday morning," says Dad. "Maybe we can start you studying this weekend. Did they give you a list of spelling words?"

"I need to check my backpack, Dad. It's out in the garage," I say, trying to change the subject. "Come on, Cole, Mom told us to get the paper."

"Why can't you go out to the driveway by yourself?" he complains. "We're not even through eating."

"Go help your sister," Mom commands.

We head out the garage door to the driveway.

"You are such a tattletale," I say, nudging Cole once we are out of earshot. "Why'd you have to tell Mom and Dad about the spelling bee?" He elbows me back.

Then we both stop in our tracks.

Three hairy pigs are running around our front yard. One scatters when it sees us. The other two squeal and head in our direction.

"Ahhhhh!" I scream, then run toward the garage, pulling Cole along with me. The pigs double back and run off.

Our front yard, which was once a smooth carpet of green, is now filled with jagged, overturned tufts of dirt. If I hadn't seen the animals, I would have sworn Cole had hopped through every inch of grass on his pogo stick. Our yelling brings Mom and Dad outside.

"What happened?" I ask, pressing as close to my father as I can get.

He whistles. "Our lawn's been attacked by wild boar."

"Wild boar!?" I exclaim.

"They dug up our yard looking for grubs and bugs to eat," Dad explains. "Food's probably been scarce for them, because we haven't had a lot of rain."

There was hardly any rain in Houston, the city we live near, this summer. The plants that wild animals that live near our neighborhood normally eat didn't grow, so they ate bushes, flowers, and even attacked small family pets for food.

I notice that the pigs dug up some of our neighbors' lawns, too.

"What are we going to do about the grass?" I ask Dad. "Will the pigs come back?"

"We'll have to have it replanted," Dad says, shaking his head. "This happened with one of our neighbors down the street, and they put a special sensor in the yard to scare the hogs off."

With all the excitement I miss my chance to ask about a pet goldfish.

We had plans to go out as a family this afternoon, but Dad tells us to go ahead without him. He will make sure we get the sensors we need to drive off the hogs. Three little pigs have put my dreams on hold.

Chapter 2

Mutton Bustin'

Three hours later, Mom, Cole and I stroll through the crowds at the Houston Rodeo.

Cole is in the first grade. Mom thinks he's as cute as can be. To me, he's a royal pain.

"Stop stepping on the back of my shoe," I demand through gritted teeth. This was the fourth time he'd bumped into me.

"Mooom, Sophie pinched me," he whines.

"If you two don't stop bickering, we're heading home," Mom warns.

We pipe down. We've been waiting for the rodeo all week. The month-long event includes carnival rides, a livestock show and concerts featuring various singers. We usually go to several activities at the rodeo before it is over, so we will probably make another trip when Dad can join us.

This morning, Mom is taking us to the Kid Kountry agriculture section that teaches about everything that goes into running a farm, from a kid's point of view. They have a birthing center where cows, sheep and pigs are born, and show baby chicks hatching from eggs. A section on plants shows how cotton grows and how it is made into cloth. There are also pony rides and a petting zoo where you can pet live goats, sheep, pigs, rabbits and other animals.

What Cole and I love best are the pig races and the Mutton Bustin' contests. Pigs of all shapes and sizes run around a track in the races, which are always fun to watch. In Mutton Bustin', smaller kids put on helmets and vests, then hold onto a sheep's wool while it runs and bucks. The child that stays on the longest wins a trophy. I'd always wanted to try Mutton Bustin', but never had the nerve. Now that I'm 10, I'm too old to try. The riders have to be from five to six years old and weigh no more than 60 pounds.

We spend at least two hours looking at all the animal booths, and even see some piglets that were born just that morning. They are no bigger than my hand, and so wiggly and cute. Their mother is named Miss Piggy.

"I wonder if they are related to the pigs that were in our yard," I joke to Mom.

After a lunch of huge, smoked turkey legs, lemonade and funnel cakes, we make our way over to the Pig Races and Mutton Bustin' tents. It looks like we missed the last pig races, but a sign says Mutton Bustin' is going to start in about 15 minutes.

"We are just about ready to begin Mutton Bustin'," says the announcer, "But we need two more riders to round out our group."

"Mommy, Mommy, I want to sign up!" says Cole, jumping up and down.

"I don't know how safe it is, honey," Mom says.

"All riders wear helmets and vests for safety," says the announcer, as if in answer to her fears.

"Please Mom. I know I can do it," Cole begs. "Last year you said I could try when I was six."

Mom nods her head yes and Cole races over to the announcer.

"Wait for us, Cole!" she says, following close behind.

"I can't believe you're letting him do this!" I say. "That's not fair! I always wanted to try Mutton Bustin' and you never let me."

"I don't remember you ever asking to do Muttin Bustin', Sophie," says Mom.

"I never did, but I always wanted to!" I respond irritably. "You let Cole do everything."

The announcer takes Cole into a holding area with about five other kids. We watch as they put on his helmet and vest.

"Hold tight to the sheep and don't let go," Mom instructs Cole, who nods his head.

"Is that thing heavy?" I ask, rapping my knuckles on the helmet.

Mom and I have to leave the back area right before the contest begins. We sit in the bleachers in the front row so we'll see all the action.

The first contestant steps forward in the ring. Her blond curls hang out of the sides of her helmet. She wears pink cowboy boots.

"Let's all welcome Lisbeth," says the announcer. "Her favorite food is chicken nuggets, and when she grows up she wants to be a fairy princess."

Lisbeth is swooped onto the back of a sheep named Lambchop and the Mutton Bustin' fun begins. Lambchop arches her back and shakes from side to side. She does not want anyone on her back. Despite all the movement, Lisbeth stays on a full 15 seconds. She curtsies for the audience, once she dusts herself off after her fall.

Taylor, the next contestant, starts crying when they try to put him on the sheep and refuses to get on, so he is taken out of the ring.

Next is Cole's turn. He looks kind of small standing there beside the sheep, but he doesn't seem scared at all.

"Let's give a big welcome to Cole," yells the announcer. "His favorite food is pizza, and when he grows up he wants to be a dentist, just like his Dad."

"I'll have to tell your father about that," smiles Mom.

Cole's sheep is named Baabara. When they place him on the sheep, Cole tries to sit up straight, but is soon leaning to the side and holding on for dear life. He makes his way halfway down the center of the ring on the back of his sheep and lasts a full 35 seconds. Mom snaps a photo of him before he falls off. The crowd of at least 200 goes wild.

"Let's hear it for Cole and his sheep, Baabara!" screams the announcer.

We go back to get him and he grins from ear to ear, showing off the gap from his missing front tooth.

"I did it, Mom! I did it!"

"Great job, honey," says Mom, giving him a hug.

She takes his helmet and vest off, and we go back out to watch the last boy get ready for his ride.

"Brandon's favorite food is barbecue ribs," says the announcer, "and he wants to be a rodeo rider when he grows up." Brandon beats Cole's time by 10 seconds. He also rips the back of his jeans while he struggles to hold onto his sheep named Baaby.

"Look, he even wore cowboy underwear," points Cole, after he notices that the briefs under Brandon's torn jeans have horses and cows on them.

"Now that's a real cowboy," laughs Mom.

When we get home, Mom shows Dad the picture of Cole hanging tight on Baabara.

"I didn't know I was raising a cowboy," he smiles, patting Cole's head.

Dad shows us where he's hooked up sensors to keep the wild pigs from coming back. A lawn service will come next week to add new grass.

The conversation turns back to the spelling bee.

"I was in a bee once when I was your age," remembers Dad. "I didn't study much, so I didn't do well. That's why I want you to make sure you review all the words carefully after you sign up Monday."

I nod my head yes and fake a smile.

I'm going to kill Cole. I had hoped to *not* sign up for the contest. Who wants to spend all their extra time studying spelling words for some silly bee? And I definitely don't want to stand up in front of all the other fifth graders and spell words. What if I miss something easy and everyone laughs?

"Bee" is a good name for this spelling contest, all right. I can think of nothing better than flying off somewhere as fast as a hornet, or stinging that bratty brother of mine!

Chapter 3

Mr. Know-It-All

My stomach is in knots the entire drive to school Monday morning. Rain pours down in buckets and the gray sky matches my mood. Today is the day I have to sign up for the spelling bee.

Cole looks out the window or thumbs through his Video Rangers handbook, which gives detailed information about all the Video Rangers characters. Last night, I forgave him for telling Mom and Dad about the spelling bee after he'd let me eat the last chocolate chip cookie left in the jar and promised to make my bed for the rest of the week.

I shift uncomfortably in my seat. My uniform shirt feels even scratchier than usual. Most of the other kids on our block go to the neighborhood school, but Mom drives us to Xavier Academy, a private school across town.

Ever since kindergarten, I've been begging to switch to the school in our subdivision so we can ride on a yellow school bus, and wear regular clothes to school instead of uniforms, like most normal people, but Mom isn't having it. "Xavier offers the best elementary and middle school educations in this area, and you'll appreciate it when you're older," she says. So, it looks like we're stuck with navy pants and skirts, polo shirts and oxfords, and loads of homework every night, at least until high school.

As she cruises into the carpool lane, Mom turns to Cole and me with a smile. "Have a great day, kids. Cole, remember to turn in that permission slip I put in your backpack for the field trip next week And don't forget to sign up for the spelling bee, Sophie."

"Okay Mom; see you later," we say. We heft our heavy backpacks from the backseat and dodge a huge puddle as we make our way into the school entrance. I turn left and Cole turns right once we enter the front door of the school. He goes to the kinder, first and second grade wing and I head toward the fifth-grade classrooms. Unlike the younger grade kids, we have actual lockers and switch classes to get us ready for middle school.

My best friend, Chloe Hopkins, runs toward me as I near Mrs. Green's room. "Hey Sophie! How was your weekend? Did you watch that new show I told you about on Saturday?"

As usual, Chloe looks super cute. She jazzed up her uniform with red, high-top tennis shoes and patterned knee socks that match the red logo on our navy school sweaters. Her long, curly black hair is pulled back with a black headband with a red silk rose on the side, and she's wearing pearl drop earrings in her pierced ears.

"We were at the rodeo while it was on, so I missed it," I say. "But I recorded it on the DVR, so I may watch it again this coming Friday." Cole and I don't watch much television during the week because we are so busy with homework and afterschool activities. If this spelling bee business turns out the way I think it will, my TV time will probably end up being even less.

After roll is called and we say the Pledge of Allegiance, Mrs. Green reminds the class of the upcoming spelling bee.

"It would be great if everyone signs up," she says. "It's a great chance for you to improve your spelling skills. The school bee is in three weeks. Regionals are a month after that. First and second place winners from each grade will represent our school there. Can I get a show of hands of those who would like study sheets?"

Several students and I raise our hands. Mrs. Green passes me eight pages of words to study with a smile.

Nathan Jones, a boy who Chloe and I secretly call "Mr. Know-It-All, because he thinks he knows the answer to everything, turns around in his seat to smirk at me once Mrs. Green goes back to her desk.

"I don't know why you are even bothering to get a list of words for the spelling bee," he says, peering through his thick glasses. "Everyone knows that *I* am going to win the school contest and then go on to the regional bee."

He's one of the smallest kids in our class, but Nathan definitely has the biggest mouth. The only reason he has friends, in my opinion, is that his dad owns a Fun Plex video game and race car center, and he often invites the other boys there for play dates.

Nathan's older sister, Jennifer, was a student at Xavier and won first place in the school and regional spelling bees for three years running before she left for high school.

"Be quiet, smarty pants," I say. "I have gotten A's on all my spelling tests this year and I can out spell you any day." I glance down at the top sheet of the list Mrs. Green has given me. "I already know most of these words on the spelling list for the bee."

"Well, I would hope you could spell the words on the first page, because those are the easy words from the list," Nathan laughs. "Look at the last sheet."

I flip through the stack of papers on my desk and see that they are ranked as easy, average and difficult. I can't pronounce most of the words I see on the difficult sheet, but I look up at my competitor with a smile. "It won't take me long to study these and learn them all," I boast, wanting to slap the smirk off Nathan's face.

"I'm going to learn those words, *and* the words from the sixth grade list in case they get through all the other words at the regionals. There's no way

18

anyone will be able to beat me," Nathan brags. Nathan isn't the best at sports, because he's so short, but ever since first grade he's been seen as one of the best students in the class, and he is always ready for a competition.

"Nathan, could you please turn around in your seat and get ready for our language review?" says Mrs. Green. He faces the front of the room and I am finally free of the smart aleck.

When the bell rings to change classes, I head out of the room without a glance at Nathan and rush to my locker. As Cole's coach says during his basketball games, it's time to go hard or go home.

There is no way I can let that know-it-all do better than me in the spelling bee. I will have to start studying tonight.

Chapter 4

Practice Makes Perfect

As soon as we get home from school and finish snack, I rush to my room to get organized for my spelling bee studies. Pencil … check. Notebook … check. Webster's Dictionary … check. Copy of the movie "Akeelah and the Bee" to watch during study breaks … check.

I also put on my study tiara. I won the bedazzled crown at a game of math jeopardy in second grade and always wear it when I study something hard. I feel like it gives me luck.

I sit down with my material on my white canopy bed and pick up the pages of words that we'll be quizzed on at the school bee. I need to memorize each word on the list so I can make sure Nathan doesn't stand a chance.

I begin to make my way through the words on the easy page. "Antler, a-n-t-l-e-r, antler; butter, b-u-t-t-e-r, butter; careful, c-a-r-e-f-u-l, careful. I get halfway through the words on the easy list when Cole comes into my room.

"I am Cole the Magnificent," he announces, touching a black top hat he wears on his head and twirling around to show off the red and black cape on his shoulders. "Want to see me do a magic trick?" He holds up a small rock. "Watch me make this object disappear."

"Not now. I'm busy studying for the spelling bee."

"I thought you didn't want to be in the bee."

"If you knew that, why did you tell Mom and Dad about it?" I ask.

"To get on your nerves."

"Boy, get out of my room before I hurt you!" I yell. Cole takes a bow and makes his way toward the door.

Five minutes after he leaves, Mom comes into my room. "What are you up to, young lady?"

"Trying to get through the easy words on my spelling list before dinner," I say.

"Well, aren't you an eager beaver. I'm happy to see you getting excited about the competition."

"I really want to beat Nathan Jones," I say, looking up from the spelling bee list. "He thinks he's so great."

"Keep up the hard work and you may do just that. Practice makes perfect."

Cole suddenly appears in the doorway to my room, not looking as "Magnificent" as he had earlier. He has a funny look on his face. His top hat is off his head and he is rubbing his left hand by his ear.

"Moooom," he says slowly with his eyes wide as saucers, "I think something's wrong."

"What happened, honey?" asks Mom, jumping up from the bed where she had been sitting beside me. "Did you break something downstairs? Are you hurt?"

"I tried to make my object disappear, like I saw Dad do, but now I can't find it."

"What object? What are you talking about?" Mom raises her voice.

Oh brother. What has this boy done now? I remember Dad was showing Cole magic tricks on Saturday. He'd pretended to pull a penny out of his ear to make it look like it had magically appeared. *I* knew that it wasn't actual magic and just a trick, but I guess Cole didn't.

"Did you stick the rock in your ear?" I ask my brother. He nods his head yes.

"Let me see," said Mom. She spends a minute looking in his ear to see if she can pull out the pebble trapped inside, with no luck. "We need to go to Dr. Lucas' office."

Great. Now how am I going to get through the easy words list before bedtime? Cole and I put on our sneakers while Mom calls the doctor's office.

She also calls Dad at his dental practice to let him know we might not be home when he gets here. I ditch my tiara and grab my school sweater in case it's cold in the doctor's office. I have a feeling this is going to be a long afternoon.

Chapter 5

A Small World

The drive to Dr. Lucas' office is uneventful. I read through words on my spelling list and Cole, paralyzed by fear, sits up straighter than I've ever seen him sit, holding his hand near his ear.

"Does your ear hurt, honey?" Mom asks sweetly, looking back at him through the car's rearview mirror.

"No, I can't feel it."

"Well, I don't ever want you to do something so crazy again!" she snaps. "I need to be getting dinner ready and your sister has schoolwork to finish. How could you do something so silly?"

Cole slumps down in his seat while Mom fusses at him about being safe for the rest of the drive.

We pull into the parking lot near the back door of our doctor's office and rush in. While Mom signs paperwork, Cole and I play the jukebox game of Pac Man that is in the waiting room. Cole beats me in five games straight. Finally, the nurse calls his name to go back to the doctor.

Mom sets her magazine down. "Come on, kids."

The nurse weighs Cole and measures his height, then takes his temperature and blood pressure. Mom answers the nurse's questions about why we came to the office and the nurse leaves the room. The ten-minute wait seems like forever. I look at the dinosaur mural on the wall and Mom scolds Cole for rolling around the room in the chair with wheels that the doctor usually sits in. Finally, Dr. Lucas walks in with another nurse.

"So, I hear we have a magician in the house," he jokes.

"I was trying to make an object disappear," says Cole weakly.

"Well, let's see if I can make it reappear," Dr. Lucas says. "Nurse Jones, hand me the tweezers."

The doctor squeezes the tool in Cole's ear, trying to get hold of the rock. "Aaaaaaaiiiiee!" my brother squeals.

"Looks like that's not going to work," says Dr. Lucas. "Let's try to flush it out."

The nurse gets some squirty thing and tells Cole to lean his head to the side. They fill his ear with water and the rock floats out.

"Thank goodness!" Mom exclaims.

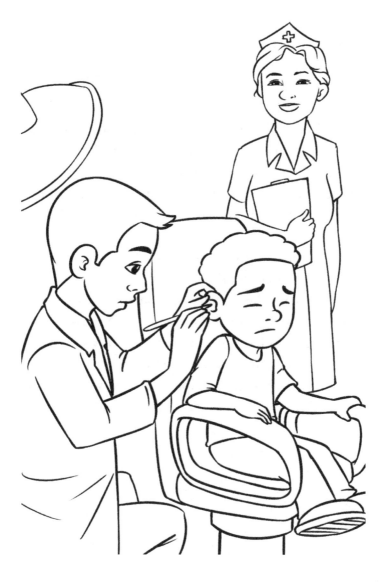

I look up from the spelling list I am studying and smile.

"If this didn't work we were going to have to send you to the Emergency Room," says Dr. Lucas.

Nurse Jones notices the logo on my school sweater. "Do you kids go to Xavier Academy? My son Nathan is a student there."

Oh, my goodness! She must be Nathan's mom. Tall, slim and pretty, she looks more like a super model than the mother of a nerdy know-it-all. Hopefully, she won't tell her son about my brother putting a rock in his ear. The teasing would never end.

"Yes, he's in my class," I say.

"It's a small world, isn't it?" says Nurse Jones, and I nod my head. She looks at my list of words. "You're studying for the spelling bee! Nathan will be in that, too. What a great experience for you kids."

"Yes, ma'am," I nod in agreement.

Mom lets us get lollipops on the way out and we head home. Wait until I tell Chloe about this.

Chapter 6

The Beat Down

"I can't believe your brother put a rock in his ear," laughs Chloe, nearly choking on her chocolate milk. "That's about as crazy as the time my sister, Nina, stuck a dime up her nose."

"I know, and the worst part about it is that Mr. Know-It-All's mom was one of the nurses in the room. She figured out we went to Xavier because I had my school sweater on."

"How embarrassing."

As if on cue, Nathan and his crew come into the cafeteria. They bump each other and rough house so much they almost drop their trays of food.

"Look the other way so they don't see us," I whisper. But it is too late. Nathan spots us and is heading our way.

"Ready for the spelling bee, Sophie?" he asks.

"Why do you care?" I say.

"I want to make sure you put extra time into going over your words, since I've been studying mine for a month. My mom told me you were struggling trying to catch up last night at the doctor's office. She said you were so busy you barely noticed when they pulled a rock out of your brother's head."

He nudges one of his friends and laughs.

"There's no way you could have studied your words for a month when we only got the list yesterday," I retort, ignoring his comments about Cole.

"Well, since my sister won the bee a couple of years ago, I already had a copy of the words from her to get a head start," he taunts.

"Don't even listen to him, Sophie," says Chloe. "Everyone knows they change the spelling bee list every year. Only the judges know what the words are."

"Be quiet, Chloe," says Nathan. "You're so scared of getting beat by me in the spelling bee that you didn't even sign up. C-A-T is too hard for you."

His buddies crack up laughing behind him.

Now he's really done it. Chloe has a learning disability called dyslexia that makes it more difficult for her to read and spell than other kids. Our kindergarten teacher noticed the problem a few years back when she couldn't spell simple words like cat and dog. Chloe has a special tutor to help her, but she takes all her regular classes with the rest of us.

Along with the dyslexia, Chloe also has a bad temper that comes out when someone makes fun of her about it. She stands up and towers over the much-shorter Nathan.

"Listen, Rock Head, I don't know what your problem is, but if you don't get out of our faces *right* now, you're going to be learning how to spell 'beat down'."

"Ooooh, she told you, man," says his friend Carlos.

Nathan tries to play it off like he isn't scared, but he can tell she is serious.

"Let's go, guys," he says, turning to leave. "I don't fight girls, but I *will* beat them at the spelling bee, and you can count on it."

They walk off.

"He's crazy," I say.

"He must really be worried that you have chance of beating him," says Chloe, "or else he wouldn't be going to all this trouble bothering you."

"Well, I'm going to try my hardest to do just that."

Chapter 7

Study Time

After the cafeteria incident, I study even harder. There is no way I can let Nathan Jones win this spelling bee. To make sure I focus, I order Cole to stay out of my room when he sees me wearing my study tiara. And I ask Chloe not to call me in the afternoons until the spelling bee is over.

It doesn't take me long to realize that this isn't as fun as they make it look on the Scripps National Spelling Bee that comes on television each year. On the national spelling bee, they show the kids spelling the words like pros.

"Spell supercalifragilisticexpialidocious," says the announcer, and the kid rattles it off like its nothing. The speller wins. His face is all over television. Everyone calls him a genius. Looks like a piece of cake.

What they *don't* show you is the hours the spellers spend learning the words. *That* part is torture.

Each day after I finish my homework, I put on my study tiara and review at least 20 words on the list I am working on. I write each word down ten times, then I practice spelling the words without looking. Once I learn those words, I add 20 more.

Dad or Mom quiz me each night, and make me repeat the words over and over again if I miss them.

"I'm getting tired of studying," I whine to Dad one night after he tells me to get my list out to review. "Maybe I should take a break."

"While you're taking a break, your competition is working," replies Dad. "You said you wanted to win this thing. I'll bet Nathan is halfway through the difficult list right now. If you want to be better than average, then you need to do more than average."

Dad tells me how striving for excellence helped him complete dental school and set up his own dental practice. Now he has his own business.

I look out the window and wistfully watch Cole throw a football with his best friend, Jeff. Why did I decide that I wanted to win!?

To make studying less boring, I try to study while I jump rope, like Akeelah did in the movie, but I keep dropping my list. And forget having my brother help me. Cole can't pronounce the words well enough to quiz me on them. He says e bony, for ebony, for example.

It looks like the good old-fashioned, but dull way of studying by sitting down at a desk and memorizing my words is the way to go.

"We're really proud of you, Sophie," Mom says after my second week of studying is over. "You made up your mind to go for it in this spelling bee and you are putting in the hard work to make sure you do your best. Whatever happens, you're a winner in my book. Dad and I have a special surprise for you and Cole this weekend that should give you a nice break from the studying," she adds.

I beg her to tell me what it is, but Mom just smiles and tells me I'll find out after school tomorrow. For once, I can't wait for the school day to begin.

Chapter 8

Granny Washington

I rush to my locker after sixth period on Friday.

"Hey girl, what are you doing this weekend?" Chloe starts in.

"I can't talk now; Mom is waiting with a big surprise."

I grab my backpack and speed-walk to the carpool line.

"This is the quickest I've ever seen you make it from class," says Mom after I slam the car door shut.

"You've got to tell me what the surprise is!" I exclaim.

Cole comes in from his carpool area and shows Mom an A paper he earned in math.

"Great job, hot shot. Now's the time to tell you the neat surprise we have planned for this weekend," Mom says as she drives down the road.

"Dad has a dental conference in Austin tomorrow and I'm joining him. Your Granny Washington is going to stay with you tonight and part of tomorrow."

Cole and I cheer, and gave each other a high five. We love it when our parents go out and leave us with a sitter. And having our grandparents stay is almost like getting an early Christmas present.

They spoil us rotten, let us buy cool things at the store and stay up way past our bedtime, and they let us eat all our favorite foods.

Grandma and Paw Paw Spencer are Mom's parents. They live in Georgia. Since it is so far away, we only see them two or three times a year when they come to visit us here in Houston, or we go to their place for holidays.

Granny Washington lives in Corpus Christi, Texas, where Dad grew up. That is about a four-hour drive from our house in Houston, so we see her more often. Granny's husband Clarence died when I was four years old and Cole was a small baby. We usually stay with her for a week in the summer, and have fun playing in the sand and waves at the beach, and visiting the Texas State Aquarium.

Though she is a grandma, Granny doesn't seem old to me. She used to be a newspaper reporter and has lots of neat friends she worked with who live all over the country.

Granny makes it easy for me to talk about things I feel funny about telling Mom and Dad, like boys who like me, or fights I have with my friends. She lets me help cook and, even though I won't admit it to my friends, I still like to cuddle in her lap.

"Granny should be here any minute," says Mom. "I'm going to go finish my packing. Your snack is in the fridge."

"The last time Granny came to visit, she promised to take us to the Children's Museum downtown," said Cole, munching on the cheese, crackers and fruit Mom had left out for us.

"Well, I'd like to visit the new doll store that opened at the mall last month," I say.

"That's not fair," cries Cole. "You know I don't want to go to the boring mall and look at yucky dolls!"

"Kids, you're not going to have Granny running all over town when she comes," says Dad, overhearing our conversation and entering the kitchen. "She needs to drive back home Sunday morning, and I don't want her to be worn out. And don't think about going to the mall, because I've already told her that she is not to buy you lots of extravagant gifts while she's here."

After Granny arrives, we both rush to give her a big hug. She wears a blue and purple jacket with a swirly paisley pattern on it. As usual, she smells delicious, like flowers and cinnamon mixed together. Mom and Dad leave contact information for the hotel where they'll be staying and hit the road.

"How are my two favorite grandkids doing?" Granny says with a smile.

"We're your only grandkids," I say, giggling.

As usual, Granny didn't come empty handed. She brought a set of bright nail polishes for me and some neat toy cars for Cole.

"Thanks Granny," we exclaim, giving her another hug.

Granny spends a few minutes catching up with us about what was going on at school. She knew a little bit about the spelling bee, because I had called her the day after I signed up and told her how Nathan had been acting.

"Sounds to me like that young man has a bit of a crush on you, Sophie," she muses. "Otherwise, why would he spend so much time worrying about what you're doing?"

"Sophie and Nathan, sitting in a tree, k-i-s-s-i-n-g," teases Cole. I pop him on the behind with a kitchen towel while Granny searches through the pantry for dinner fixings.

She makes meatballs and spaghetti, which is one of our favorites. Both of us gobble up every bit of food on our plates. When dinner is finished, Cole shows Granny some of his drawings and I study my spelling lists. About an hour later, Mom and Dad call to let us know they made it safely to Austin.

Cole and settle down to watch a movie. As usual, we stay up way past our bedtime, laughing and talking with Granny for an hour or so after the movie ends.

She tells us funny stories about how she used to trick her younger brother and sister into giving her their coins when she was little. She'd tell them that a nickel was worth more than a dime because it was bigger. Then she tells us about some of the famous people she interviewed when she was a journalist, like the writer Maya Angelou, and Dr. Mae Jemison, the first African-American female astronaut.

Before she tucks us into our beds that night, Granny reads us a story from an Aesop's Fable book she'd bought us a few years earlier. Cole drifts off to sleep before the story is over.

I share some of my fears about the upcoming spelling bee with Granny.

"Nathan has lists of words from the times when his sister was in the spelling bees, so he has a head start over me. What if I don't know some of the words, since I haven't been studying as long?"

"I wouldn't even worry about that, Sophie," she says. "Just like in the story we finished reading about the tortoise and the hare, slow and steady wins the race. Focus on your own studying. Don't worry about what he's doing."

I smile with contentment as I drift off to sleep. Having grandparents visit is the best.

Chapter 9

R-E-S-P-E-C-T

Time whizzes by between the day I got my spelling list and the actual school bee. I stay as far away from Nathan as possible, like Granny Washington suggested, so I won't waste any study time listening to his teasing.

I review my list every day after school and make it through all the words. Dad promises me a surprise gift if I win. He and Mom quiz me whenever they can, and Cole even puts down his Video Rangers book to try and help me study words on the way to school each morning.

"Here we go," I think as I line up with ten other fifth graders to compete. The school bee is being held in Xavier's library and parents aren't allowed.

The library is a small room with flat green carpet on the floor. I used to pretend I was sitting in a meadow in the woods when we'd come here for story time in kindergarten. We stand in the front of the room and the students just watching sit across from us in chairs around long tables.

Nathan sports a sweater vest, along with his school oxford and navy pants, and some glasses that I've never seen him wear. I wear ribbons with my usual ponytails, and I'm wearing my nicest skirt.

I try to avoid Nathan on the way to the library, but no such luck. "Getting nervous, Sophie?" he teases. "You should be. I know every word on this spelling list. There's no way you can beat me. I even know all the words from the sixth-grade list."

"Whatever," I say, flipping out my hand to dismiss him. "I know all the words too, and they aren't even going to give us the sixth-grade words today anyway."

"We'll see what happens," he says. We enter the room and he high fives his friends, Carlos and Jack.

I scope out the competition. Immediately, I rule out three of the kids as nothing to worry about.

Joshua Smith, Cynthia Michaelson and Jose Cruz usually get average grades in spelling, and rarely study for anything. Their parents must have made them sign up.

Caleb Bishop, Olivia Dunbar, Josiah Joseph and Kennedy Emmanuel are all decent students who might do alright if they have studied.

Mariama Asante is a mystery. Her family moved to Houston from Nigeria this past summer, so she is new to our school. I haven't had any classes with her. She may give me a run for my money if I don't watch out.

And last, but not least, Mr. Know-It-All, Nathan Jones, whose main goal in life is to win this contest and get on my last nerve.

"I will say the word to you once, then I'll say the word in a sentence," says Mrs. Green. "You may ask for a definition of the word if you need to know the meaning. You will then say the word, spell it, and finally say the word again. If you say any of the letters incorrectly, you must leave the contest. The top two spellers will go on to represent Xavier in the regional bee. Best of luck to you all."

My heart pounds in my chest and my hands feel cold. Mrs. Green walks to the front of the line. Mariama Asante is first and I am fifth. Nathan is the last person in the row.

I look out at the audience. Chloe, who is sitting in the front row of tables lined up in the library, gives me a smile. The thirty or so fifth graders who aren't competing in the contest are all there to watch the big event. Our assistant principal, Mr. Grayson, warns them to be extra quiet once the spelling bee begins or get put in detention later in the week.

"The first word is born," says Mrs. Green. "The calf was born in the barn."

"Born," says Mariama. "B-o-r-n, born."

"That is correct," Mrs. Green replies.

She goes on to give words to Joshua, Cynthia and Jose. As I expected, they don't last long. Joshua spells poet, p-o-i-t, and Cynthia spells thirst, t-h-e-r-s-t. Jose's downfall comes with the word chain, which he spells c-h-a-y-n-e. Olivia misses the word jiffy, which surprises me, since I know she spelled it correctly on our spelling test a few weeks ago. She must be really nervous. Next, it is my turn. "Respect," said Mrs. Green. "Do a good job and you will command respect."

"Respect," I say, smiling. "R-e-s-p-e-c-t, respect." Once I get through my first word, I feel my belly get warm and the jitters go away. I am on my way to winning this thing!

I glance at Nathan out of the corner of my eye after I finish, but he doesn't react. We go through about six rounds after that with no one missing a word. Then they start dropping like flies.

"Oath," Mrs. Green says to Kennedy. "The president took an oath of office."

"O-a-f-t-h," she answers slowly.

"I'm sorry, Kennedy, that is incorrect," Mrs. Green says. "Oath is spelled o-a-t-h."

Kennedy drops her head and takes her seat, and the bee continues with kids misspelling words every few minutes. Fifteen minutes later, it is between me, Mariama and Nathan.

"Terse," Mrs. Green says to me. "The angry man was terse with the clerk."

"Terse, t-e-r-s-e, terse," I spell back.

"Adjacent," Mrs. Green says to Mariama. "The school is adjacent to the gymnasium."

"May I get a definition please?" Mariama asks.

"Adjacent means being nearby, or in close proximity," says Mrs. Green.

"Adjacent, a-j-a-c-e-n-t, adjacent," says Mariama.

"I'm sorry, but you have spelled the word incorrectly," Mrs. Green says. "You may take a seat."

Mr. Know-It-All and I are now the last kids standing.

"Great job for making it this far," says Mrs. Green. "You are our first and second place winners and will represent Xavier in the regional spelling bee. We will now do our final spell-off to determine who will be the champion of the school bee."

"Go Sophie!" yells Chloe, ducking her head in the crowd so that the principal can't see her.

My knees begin to knock and my hands feel sweaty. We go through five more rounds, then Mrs. Green gives Nathan the word "magistrate".

"Magistrate, m-a-g-i-s-t-r-a-i-g-h-t, magistrate," he says, shifting his weight from side to side.

I can't believe it, Mr.-Know-It-All made a mistake.

"I'm sorry, Nathan, but that is incorrect," says Mrs. Green. "Sophie, I'd like you to spell magistrate. If you spell that word correctly, I will give you another word to spell to be named the champion."

Nathan glares at me, but I ignore him. "Magistrate, m-a-g-i-s-t-r-a-t-e, magistrate," I carefully spell.

"That is correct," says Mrs. Green. "The word for the championship is intrigue. The mystery was full of intrigue."

"Intrigue," I say. "I-n-t-r-i-g-u-e, intrigue."

"That is correct," says Mrs. Green as the kids in the library go wild. They cheer, clap and jump out of their seats. They are happy that I won, and even happier that they can stop sitting quietly.

I can't believe it. I am champion of the Xavier Academy fifth-grade spelling bee. All my hard work paid off!

Nathan comes up and shakes my hand. "Good job, Sophie, but don't count me out, because *I* will be at the regional competition and I *will* beat you there. I took it easy on you today."

"Yeah right, Nathan," I say, rolling my eyes. That boy is too much. Chloe rushes up and gives me a big hug. "Way to go, spelling champion!" she cheers.

Then Mrs. Green hands me a trophy with a cute bobble head bee on it that says: "First Place Winner." She pulls me and Nathan aside to take pictures with our trophies and the principal. This is the best day ever! I can't wait to tell Mom and Dad.

Chapter 10

Oh Brother

When Mom picks me up from school that day, I am all smiles.

"I won! I won!" I say, waving my bee trophy in the air. I meant to pretend I had lost, and then give Mom the good news, but I can't hold it in.

"I'm so proud of you, sweetie! Wait until we tell your dad!" Mom dials Dad's office on her cell phone before the car pool line starts moving and we both talk to him through the Bluetooth feature in the car.

"That's great news, Princess," he says. "I knew you could do it. What's the next step?"

I explain to him that I will be in the regional bee a month from now, and I need to keep reviewing the words so they'll be fresh in my mind. Mrs. Green gave me more words to study that could be included in the regional bee.

"Well, we'll help you in any way we can, sweetheart," said Dad. "You see how hard work pays off? Looks like I need to take you out to get that surprise I promised you this weekend."

I grin with excitement.

"What surprise are you getting me, Dad? Is it something I can buy at the mall?"

"You'll see when we get it, sweetheart," he teases.

We pull around to the pickup area for the lower school to get Cole. His teacher, Mrs. Brandt, comes to the passenger side window as Cole gets in the back of the car. He slumps his shoulders.

"Hi, Mrs. Brandt, how are you?" asks Mom.

"Things are alright with me, Mrs. Washington, but I want to let you know that Cole has not been focusing well in school these past few days," she says. "He's been daydreaming when we are going over assignments in class, and yesterday he was doodling on construction paper when I was teaching a new math lesson. If this continues, his grades may go down, so I want to make you aware."

"Thanks for letting me know what is going on, Mrs. Brandt," says Mom, glancing in the backseat towards a wide-eyed Cole. "Be assured that this problem won't continue."

Having a brother is the pits. Mom spends most of the ride home talking to Cole about why he should be responsible and pay attention in class. Today is *my* day, and all the attention should be on *me*. Yet here I am again, listening to the brat of the century get in trouble.

Cole hasn't even congratulated me on winning the spelling bee. He's probably just jealous. I watch him squirm in his seat as Mom goes on and on.

When we get home, I head straight to my room and put on my princess tiara. I feel like royalty, so why not dress like it? All the attention is on Cole for now, but soon everyone will recognize me for the queen I really am.

Downstairs, Mom seems to have settled down about Cole's teacher's comments. Then I hear her calling Grandma and Paw Paw and Granny Washington to tell them my good news. She opens cabinets and gets out pots and pans to get dinner ready.

A few minutes later, Cole walks in my room holding something behind his back.

"What do you want now, Rock Head?" I ask him. "I should kick you out of here for getting Mom mad. Why don't you just behave in school? And what's that you're holding?"

"Just something I made for you," he says, sticking out a yellow sheet of paper.

"Let me see." On the paper is a drawing of a lady bee wearing a skirt and a crown. 'Congradulations Sophie!' it reads.

"Thanks, Cole," I said. "This is so good! When did you make it?"

"Yesterday," he said. "I knew you would win."

I remember once Dad said Cole has great focus when he does his artwork. He said Cole is so good because he is able to tune out everything around him when he is working.

"Is this what you were doing in school when your teacher was explaining things?" I ask.

He nods his head yes. "I'm glad you won the bee."

"I really like the picture, Cole." I hang it on my dresser mirror. Then I give Cole a hug, and for the first time in a long time, he hugs me back.

Sometimes having a little brother isn't so bad.

Chapter 11

Fun Plex

Three hours of video games, bumper cars, and seven-year-old boys hyper on candy and cake. Nathan Jones and his father everywhere I turn. It's a birthday party at Fun Plex, and it's my worst nightmare come true.

Cole's best friend, Jeff, invited him and all the boys from his first-grade class to his seventh birthday party. My brother has been looking forward to the big event for the past two weeks.

"Do I have to go, too?" I whine as Mom picks up her car keys.

"I'm sorry, sweetie, but I've planned to attend this ladies lunch at our church for the last month and kids aren't allowed," she explains. "Why are you so against going to Fun Plex? You used to love that place."

"That's before I met that icky Nathan Jones and realized that his father is the owner," I say. "He's there anytime you go, and I don't want to listen to him teasing me about the spelling bee. And other times I've gone to Fun Plex with *my* friends, not Cole's."

"Sophie, I think you're worrying for nothing," Mom says. "Go to the party and enjoy yourself, and I'll see you when I get back."

Mom slides on her brown suede jacket and brown leather boots, grabs her purse and heads out the door.

Cole and Dad join me in the foyer and we make our way to the car.

I listen to my favorite songs on the radio on the way to Fun Plex and ignore the thoughts of the bad time to come. Ten minutes later, we pull into the game center's parking lot, then follow the groups of happy kids and tired-looking parents inside.

"Hey Cole!" Jeff runs up to him and gives him a chest bump.

"Happy Birthday, Jeff!" Cole replies.

When we join the rest of the group, Dad explains why I'm at the party to Jeff's mother, and offers to pay my way.

How embarrassing! Not only am I at a party for babies, but my Dad has to pay for me to be here.

"Sophie is more than welcome at the party; there's no need to pay for her," Jeff's mom says.

We enter the main hall to get tokens for video games and bumper cars.

That's when my worst fear comes true. Guess who's at the front counter helping out? Nathan Jones. He's wearing a Fun Plex t-shirt and jeans, and looks even scrawnier than he does in his school uniform.

"Hey Sophie," he says, peering out of his dark-rimmed glasses. "Coming to spy on the competition?"

"I'm not spying on anyone, Nathan, just having fun at a party with friends." I quickly get my tokens and hurry to catch up with the rest of the group at the video games. I hope that Nathan doesn't realize I'm spending my Saturday afternoon with a bunch of seven-year-olds.

Nathan stays busy behind the counter with his dad, so I breathe a sigh of relief that I won't have to speak to him the rest of my time at Fun Plex. I end up having a good time at the party.

Jeff's older sister Ava, who is in fourth grade, is here. We play air hockey and video games together, and have a blast on the bumper cars. Knocking Cole and Jeff's fire engine red cars into the side of the bumper car area with my blue one is especially fun. I use half my tokens on that.

The Fun Plex pizza and birthday cake tastes even better than I remember it being at the party I came to last year.

On the way out, I see Nathan sorting through plastic spoons and forks.

"Boy, get back here and put those napkins out like I told you!" his father yells from a back room.

Nathan scurries to find the napkins and trips over a box of tokens. He looks around to make sure no one sees him and quickly bends to pick up the wayward tokens before his dad finds out. If he wasn't such a jerk, I'd kind of feel sorry for him.

Cole, Dad and I make our way out to the parking lot.

"Thanks for taking us to the party, Dad," says Cole. "I had a lot of fun."

"Me too," I say, sliding into my seat after we make it to the car.

"Well, the fun is not over yet for you, Sophie," says Dad. "Remember, I promised to get a special surprise for you for winning the spelling bee."

"Yay! What is it?" I ask, bouncing up and down in my seat.

"We're on our way now."

Chapter 12

Goldy

Ten minutes later, we pull into the parking lot of a pet store.

I start screaming. "I can't believe you're going to let me get a fish, Dad. I am soooo excited!"

"Well, you proved that you can stick to a task and be responsible, Sophie," said Dad. "And your hard work deserves a reward."

Once we enter the store, I head straight to a big fish tank in the back. Fish of every color swim to and fro. There are so many choices; I can't make up my mind.

"What about that one, Sophie?" Cole points out an orange and black-striped fish. "It looks like Nemo. Or what about the blue fish that reminds you of water at the beach?"

I watch the dazzling swirl of color for about five minutes, then finally settle on a medium-sized, golden-colored fish with large black eyes.

"That's the one I want," I say, pointing him out.

The store worker scoops him out with a fish net and dumps him in a plastic bag. Next, we buy a small fish bowl and decorative rocks and plants to put in the bowl.

"Use this food to feed your fish," says the pet store worker, handing me a pill-box sized container. "You should also buy this cleaning liquid to use when you change the water out in your bowl each week."

"What are you going to name your fish?" Dad asks as we are on the way home.

I peer at him for a second through the plastic bag. "I think I'll call him Goldy."

The pet store workers said we have to wait overnight until the water is a certain temperature before we add the fish. I put in the rocks and plants, and then fill the bowl with water and add some of the liquid cleaner. Goldy will stay in his plastic bag of water until morning, when I can put him in his new home.

Mom is surprised when she comes home from her meeting and sees the fish.

"Though it's a small pet, it's still a responsibility, Sophie," she stresses. "You need to make sure to feed him each morning and keep his bowl clean every week so he'll stay healthy."

"Don't worry, Mom. I can do it."

Bright and early the next morning, I transfer Goldy to his new fish bowl. Then I pick up the small jar of fish food and pinch out a few granules for his daily meal.

The fish food stinks, but it must be good, because Goldy swims to the top of the bowl and gobbles it up.

"Get back!" I yell as Cole sneaks in from around the counter and sticks his face as close to the fishbowl as he can get without touching it. The glass from the bowl magnifies his close-cut haircut, so it resembles a 1970s-style afro. His big, brown eyes look huge.

I shove Cole toward the kitchen table and hold my arms out in defense of the fish. Cole backs up and heads for the family room with a scowl on his face. "I'm just trying to see if he's hungry," he says, sticking out his tongue.

"Even if he *is* hungry, you know you're not allowed to feed him or bother him, so back off," I snap.

Dad walks into the kitchen. "Cole, let your sister enjoy her new fish by herself for a while. When you are a little older we may get you your own pet to take care of."

"If I do get my own fish I won't be so stingy with it like Sophie is!" he says, turning on Video Rangers.

Maybe I *will* share with Cole later. But right now, I'm happy to spend time by myself with my very own pet.

Chapter 13

Odd Girl Out

When I walk into the classroom on Monday, I groan. Mrs. Green is out sick, so we have a substitute: Mr. Brownlee.

He subbed for us last year and it was a disaster. Mr. Brownlee gave extra work our regular teachers didn't assign. He made each kid stand in front of the class and tell about their favorite book. My mind had gone blank on my turn and I'd said, "Goodnight Moon," which had everyone calling me a baby for days.

Nathan and his friends nicknamed him Mr. Brown Bear behind his back, because Mr. Brownlee looks like a furry grizzly. He has a thick mustache, hairy arms and a round, pot belly.

"Good morning, class," Mr. Brownlee greets us with his deep baritone voice. "Today we're going to talk about Spirit Week and choices you have for the dress-up contests. Before that, let's discuss your favorite literature. We had so much fun with that last time I was here."

"Not again!" Chloe whines from her desk in the back.

At least we get to spend time learning about Spirit Week afterwards, I think. Spirit Week is the time that leads up to Xavier's basketball game against our rival, the Whitlock School. There is a pep rally, a hall decorating contest, and each day we can wear special outfits.

Monday is Crazy Hat Day, Tuesday is Pajama Day, Wednesday is Twin Day, Thursday is College Jersey Day, and Friday is Blue and Red Day, when we wear our school colors.

Nathan Jones raises his hand. "I'd like to tell about my favorite book," he says. Mr. Brownlee nods his head for him to begin and Nathan walks to the front of the classroom.

"My favorite book is 'Brown Bear, Brown Bear' by Eric Carle," he says.

I hear his friends, Carlos and Jack, snickering. I start coughing to keep myself from cracking up.

"I love the book so much, I have it memorized." He clears his throat. "Brown bear, brown bear, what do you see? I see a green frog looking at me. Brown bear, brown bear, what do you see? I see a black mustache looking at me. Brown bear, brown bear, what do you see? I see a fat round tummy looking at me."

The back half of the room howls with laugher.

"That's enough, Nathan," Mr. Brownlee shouts over the commotion. "You kids should be ashamed of yourselves for making fun of the book your classmate chose."

Mr. Brownlee has obviously never read "Brown Bear Brown Bear" or he'd know Nathan was making fun of him. The book teaches about colors and says nothing about bellies or mustaches.

Once we've settled down, a few other students talk about books they've read recently. Then the topic turns to Spirit Week.

"This is your chance to show your Xavier Rockets spirit and dress out of uniform for a change," Mr. Brownlee says. "Since Twin Day is a group activity, you may select your twin this morning."

I turn around to find Chloe, who gives me a thumbs-up sign. It is nice having a best friend who you know you can count on.

She comes over to my desk and we brainstorm ideas. My other classmates mill around the room to choose their twins.

I notice Mariama sitting alone at her desk. She is new to our school this year, so she doesn't have any close friends in the class. Some people think she is weird, because she speaks with a funny accent and wears African clothes sometimes, but she seems nice. And I know she is very smart after seeing her in action at the school spelling bee.

There are 21 kids in our home room: 10 boys and 11 girls. This makes her the odd person out when pairs are made.

Chloe suggests we style our hair in Mohawks like a teen star she saw in a video recently. "We can shake our hair around, and maybe even bring in guitars!"

"Do you think that Mariama has a partner?" I interrupt.

"I don't know," Chloe, looks across the room. "It doesn't look like anyone asked her to be their twin."

"Maybe we should," I suggest.

"We could see," says Chloe doubtfully.

I make my way to her desk. "Mariama, would you like to be partners with me and Chloe?"

"I don't know," she says, holding back tears. "Three isn't a twin."

I think for a minute. "Maybe we can be triplets. Let's ask Mr. Brownlee."

We go to Mr. Brownlee's desk and explain our plan. "Sounds like an excellent solution," he says.

Back at my desk, we try to come up with ideas for our trio. "What about the Three Musketeers?" suggests Mariama.

"No, those are all men. I don't want to be a boy character," Chloe says.

Nathan and Jose whisper something about dressing up as brothers from a popular video game. I look around the room. Most of our other classmates also have their plans in place.

"Write the group you plan to be on this sheet I'm passing around and I'll leave it for Mrs. Green," says Mr. Brownlee. The bell rings for us to head to our first period class.

"Oh no! We still don't have an idea," says Mariama. "If you had stuck with twins and not included me, you could have come up with something."

"Wait a minute. I have a perfect idea!" Chloe exclaims.

Chapter 14

African Queens

"What is it?" ask Mariama and I in unison.

"We'll be African queens and wear some of Mariama's outfits from Nigeria!" Chloe enthuses. "We'll really stand out from the crowd with those on."

"That sounds like a good idea," I say uncertainly, "but where will we get the clothes?"

The list comes around and I write "African Queens" under our names. The three of us move out of the room to our lockers.

"My mother sews," offers Mariama, getting excited. "I'm sure she could make us some boubou by Monday."

Boubou? That doesn't sound like anything I want to wear. Chloe must be thinking the same thing.

"What's a boubou?" she asks, scrunching up her nose.

"Boubou are clothes we wear in Nigeria," Mariama explains.

I remember seeing Mariama at the grocery store the weekend after school started. She wore a flowing, pink cotton gown. The loose shift fell to her ankles and was trimmed at the bottom and on the sleeves with beige and brown shells. Mom had called them cowrie beads and said they were used as money in Africa long ago.

Mariama's hair was covered with a cute pink scarf that day that had a swirly yellow and brown pattern on it, and was tied in a knot in front.

"Let's meet after school and ask my mom if she'll make them," she suggests.

When Mariama's mother comes to get her at pickup, we run to her to explain our idea. Mrs. Asante tells us that she will be happy to make us the outfits. I am bubbling over to tell Mom and Dad about our plan.

Chapter 15

Boubou and Broccoli

That night at dinner, I share our Twin Day idea.

"Mariama's mother is making us special African boubou gowns so we'll match," I explain to Mom and Dad. "I hope they are bright and colorful."

"What a great chance for you to learn something about African culture," says Dad.

"Boo boo!" laughs Cole hysterically. "You're going to wear boo boo for Twin Day?" He starts to tease me with a chant. "Sophie's going cuckoo. She's going to wear some boo boo."

"That's enough, Cole," says Mom sternly. "Stop that nasty talk at the table this instant. Sophie explained to you that a boubou is an African gown. Now, let's get ready to eat."

Mom sets down serving dishes at the table, and Cole and I look at each other in dismay. We can tell that smell anywhere. We are having broccoli, our least favorite vegetable, and Dad and Mom always make us eat some.

"Not broccoli and cheese again, Mom!" moans Cole, biting into his baked chicken leg after we'd said grace. "It's so yucky."

Mom scoops us both a big spoonful of the glop.

"Pipe down and eat your dinner," says Dad. He turns to tell Mom about something that happened at his dental practice today.

Being a dentist might sound boring, but Dad has funny stories to tell us almost every day. Once, a little girl bit him because his office didn't give out lollipops as treats. Another time, a patient fell asleep and started snoring while getting his teeth cleaned.

"Dr. Montrose came in for his regular checkup and the hygienist, Jean noticed, something unusual during his cleaning," Dad says. "His teeth were stained a greenish tint. Jean called me in and I'd never seen anything like it in my 15 years of practice."

"What was it?" Mom asks.

"Turns out he'd been on a vegetarian diet," says Dad. "Eating salads and green vegetables every day turned his teeth green."

"That's why we don't need to eat this nasty broccoli," says Cole.

I nod my head in agreement.

"I doubt the amount of vegetables you two eat is enough to turn your teeth any color," Mom says.

"Well, I guess eating broccoli is better than wearing boo boo like Sophie will be doing at Twin Day," Cole starts in again.

Dad cuts his eyes at him.

"Young man, you heard your mother tell you to stop the first time, didn't you? Don't make me step in."

"Yes, sir," says Cole, squinching up his face as he tries to swallow his broccoli without tasting it.

At school the next day, Mariama shows us some samples of the yellow, bright blue, and red cotton fabric her mom brought for our boubou. She is also going to make us head wraps called gele.

"We're going to look like real African princesses!" Chloe exclaims.

We decide to wear black sandals on our feet to complete our look.

Spirit Week turns out to be even more exciting than it was in fourth grade. Mom lets Cole and me dress up for all the activities, and we have a great time at the pep rallies and other events.

The highlight of the week is Twin Day. When Mariama, Chloe and I show up in our matching boubou and gele, everyone ooohs and ahhs.

"This is one of the most unique costumes I've seen on Twin Day," says Mrs. Green. She has us twirl around and model for the class. "Kudos for your creativity."

We win first place for the Twin Contest for the fifth grade, though some eighth graders who dressed as Thing 1 and Thing 2 from the Dr. Seuss books get the overall first prize.

The Xavier Rockets lose to the Whitlock Warriors 46-52 at the big game, but my friends and I agree that this Spirit Week topped them all.

Chapter 16

See You Later Alligator

One Sunday afternoon after dinner, Dad suggests we go on a bike ride. Cole and I are so excited that we jump up from our seats without clearing our plates from the table.

"Yay, I love riding my bike!" my brother exclaims, heading to get his tennis shoes. I run behind him.

"Hold on a minute, young man and young lady," says Mom. "You're not riding anywhere until you help clean up this kitchen."

Cole clears the table while I sweep the floor. Then we both help Mom wipe down the counters and table, and load the dishwasher.

It has been a few weeks since we've ridden our bikes beyond our street, so Dad fills our tires with air and raises Cole's bike seat while we clean up things from dinner.

After we finish up in the kitchen, we all gather in the garage and are ready to go. It is the perfect weather for riding. The late-day sky is blue and clear, and the lowering sun cools off the usual Texas fall heat and humidity.

Cole and I put on our riding helmets and we take off, he on his red and black bike, and I on my pink and white one.

"Slow down, kids!" yells Dad. "Let's stick together until we get past the main intersection."

We glide until we reach a stop sign at the end of the block, where we wait for Mom and Dad. Once they catch up and we see the coast is clear, Cole and I take off full force down the sidewalk beside the main road.

I feel like I'm flying. My pigtails stream behind me, and my loose, white and yellow striped t-shirt flaps in the breeze.

Mom is gaining ground and Dad brings up the rear. Dad pushes a gear he calls the "Magic Turbo Boost" and speeds past me and Cole. We pedal furiously to keep up.

"Catch me if you can!" Dad says, laughing. He slows down and we finally catch up.

"Can we go to the creek, Dad?" Cole puffs, easing up beside him. The small stream is an area we often pass on our way over a bridge that leads to the other side of our subdivision.

"Can we get ice cream when we're done?" I chime in, mentioning the neighborhood ice cream shop we sometimes stop at during our family outings.

"We'll see," says Mom. "First, let's make it to the creek area."

I notice the creek water is higher than usual because we've had some rain the past few days. Cole rides off the path and pulls his bike as close to the creek bank as he dares without getting in trouble.

Suddenly, Mom shrieks. She points out her hand toward the opposite side of the creek.

Sunning himself on the creek bank is an eight-foot-long alligator.

"Move back here where we are, son," commands Dad in a stern voice. Cole eases himself and his bike back to the group.

The alligator lifts his head. Cole stumbles and drops his bike.

"Hurry Cole," I hiss.

He gets his bike up and makes his way back to the rest of us.

"Will it eat us?" he whispers.

"We're not staying to find out," says Dad. "Let's go."

Dad gestures for Cole and me to get in front of him and Mom, and we all ride like the wind away from the creek area toward the community shops.

The alligator doesn't follow us.

"Looks like we need a snack break to calm our nerves," says Mom once we near the ice cream place.

"Yay!" Cole and I cheer. We enter the shop and all order cones.

"Why are there alligators so near our neighborhood?" I ask Dad in between licks of my favorite ice cream flavor, Rocky Road.

"The alligators were here in the creeks long before this subdivision was built," he explains. "They are harmless, as long as we stay away from them and avoid places where they have nests. They might attack someone if they got near their babies."

Our eyes get wide.

"But they'd have to watch out for me and Dad, because we'd put a hurting on a 'gator if it tried to do anything to either or you," chimes in Mom.

We avoid the creek on the way home and ride through some of the neighborhood streets.

As we get ready for bed that night, Cole and I agree that we can't wait to tell our friends about our bike riding adventures.

"See you later, alligator," I say before heading to my room.

"After a while, crocodile," Cole shouts back.

Chapter 17

Regionals

"Wish me luck, Goldy," I say as I give my pet fish his breakfast before sitting down for my own.

It is the day of the regional bee, so even though it is the middle of a school week, Mom makes me a hot breakfast.

"Remember to keep your focus and stay calm while you're spelling each word," she coaches. "You have studied those lists hundreds of times, so the only thing that can mess you up is your own nerves."

"Yes ma'am," I say between bites of buttermilk biscuit. I smooth my hand down the front of my school uniform skirt and am extra careful not to get grape jelly on my school shirt.

Dad gave me his best wishes before he left for work earlier that morning, and promised me another special surprise if I did well at regionals. I look over at Goldy. It was funny how my view of the contest has changed in just a few short weeks.

In the beginning, the word "bee," was as welcome to me as an insect sting. Now, I am in it to win it! My family and my school will be so proud if I win. And I will be proud of myself. Xavier hasn't had a student place first at regionals since Nathan's sister Jennifer left for high school a couple of years ago.

Mom has to help out at Dad's dental office this morning because his normal receptionist is sick, so she drops Cole and me off at school. I'm going to the regional competition in the school van with Mrs. Green and the other Xavier spellers.

I pile into the white school van with "Xavier" written on the side in navy blue letters. Nathan's mom is late dropping him off, so he slides into the only seat left in the van beside me when he finally gets in.

"Hey Sophie, ready to lose?" he asks.

"I should be asking you that, *alternate*," I say.

"Well, it's a whole new ball game at regionals," says Nathan. "They don't care whether you won at Xavier or not. You'll just be one of the kids spelling. Just like me."

"Whatever," I say, determined to ignore this pest for the rest of the drive to regionals.

Thankfully, the community center where it is held is only a fifteen-minute drive, so I don't have too long to listen to Mr. Know-It-All.

Once we get there, we all follow Mrs. Green to the registration desk to be signed in. A few kids from Xavier arrived earlier, because their parents drove them. I wish Mom was here, though I won't admit it to her. I usually tell her that she embarrasses me.

There are at least two hundred other kids and their parents in the main auditorium. Spellers are from third grade to eighth. All of us from Xavier have on our nicest school uniform outfits, but I notice that some of the other kids wear jeans.

After everyone registers, one of the bee coordinators named Ruthie McGee steps to the microphone in the front of the room.

"Welcome to the Houston Central Regional Spelling Bee Championships! I'm sure all of you are very excited to have made it this far."

"We will divide the students into rooms by grade. Only the judges will be allowed in these rooms, no parents or teachers. Once you hear your grade called, follow your group proctor to the room where you will be competing.

"We expect the contests to be complete by noon, when we'll hand out award medals and ribbons and have a spell down for those who may be going to the state competition."

Spell down? State competition? No one had told me about that. Now I feel even more nervous. Oh well, I'll just focus on getting through this part, like Mom and Dad told me.

I hear my grade called out by a judge with a sign that says Room 105 and rise from my seat. Let the games begin.

Chapter 18

Room 105

I don't want to be bothered with Nathan, so I walk slowly in the line to lag behind him. I count 26 other kids who we'll be competing against.

A tall man with a beard stands up.

"Welcome to the spelling bee regionals. My name is Bob Jones and I will be reading the words," he announces in a newscaster voice. "Ms. Vincent here beside me will write down each word I say and tape record the bee in case there are any questions later."

In this bee, we sit in a chair until our names are called; next we stand up and spell our word. If we miss a word, we'll be out of the contest and have to sit in chairs in the back of the room.

Nathan is in the first row and I am number 12 in the group. This bee is different from Xavier's because it is obvious that all of the students have studied. We go at least five rounds before anyone messes up, and that seems like it is from nerves more than not knowing how to spell the word. A few of them have been competing in the regional competition since they were in third grade. They seem like pros.

By the time we make it to the middle of the "average" list, I'm sweating. What if Nathan is right and they do get through all the fifth-grade words I've studied and go to the sixth-grade list? I wasn't able to get a copy of those words.

We get toward the beginning of the "difficult" list and some cracks begin to show in the armor of some of my competitors. An Indian boy named Sanjay misses the word "beguiling," then another girl misses "guacamole." There are seven of us left in the competition.

It's my turn again. "Symmetrical," says the proctor. I am happy I get that word because I remember studying it.

"Symmetrical," I said. "S-y-m-m-e-t-r-i-c-a-l, symmetrical."

The seven of us battle on for ten more minutes. Then the time keeper whispers something to the main judge.

"You all are some of best spellers we've had in years," she says. "Since they want us to finish up by noon, and you are doing so well, we are going to go to our Wildcard list."

Wildcard list? What's that? The judges pull out a stack of papers from a box on the floor. It doesn't take me long to figure it out. The judge starts naming words that I've never heard in my life, and my competitors begin to take seats in the back one by one. I am happy I didn't waste my time studying the sixth-grade list like Nathan did, because it doesn't look like any of these words are from there.

It is Nathan's turn again. "Potpourri," says the proctor. "Grandmother put potpourri in the linen closet."

"Potpourri," says Nathan. "P-o-t-p-o-u-r-r-i, potpourri."

"That is correct," said the proctor.

I'm impressed. There is no way I would have gotten that word right. A couple of other kids fall by the wayside and now it is between me, Nathan and a red-haired girl with braces and freckles all over her face named Lucy.

"Conscientious," says the proctor to Lucy. "The conscientious student spent many hours preparing for his test."

"Conscientious, c-o-n-t-i-e-n-c-i-o-u-s, conscientious," she spells.

"I'm sorry, but that is incorrect," says the proctor.

It is now my turn. I'm not sure how to spell it, but I think I've seen this word written down before.

"Conscientious, c-o-n-t-i-e-n-t-i-o-u-s," I spell.

"I'm sorry, but that is also incorrect," the judge says.

Oh, no, Nathan might beat me! Why did we have to go to the Wildcard words!?

Chapter 19

V-I-C-T-O-R-Y

It's now Nathan's turn to spell conscientious. He doesn't look as sure of himself as he did when he was teasing me. I notice him shifting from side to side like he did when I beat him at the school bee, so that is a good sign.

"Conscientious," he says. "C-o-n-s-i-e-n-t-i-o-u-s."

"I'm sorry, Nathan, but that is also incorrect," says the judge.

We go through a couple more rounds and none of us misses a word.

Then the judge announces another round that will start with Nathan.

She looks down at the list. "Please spell camouflage. The reptile can camouflage himself from his enemies by changing colors."

Camouflage. Whew, that is a word that we talked about just last week in history class when we were learning about the United States Army. I think I can remember it if I get a chance.

"Camouflage," spells Nathan. "C-a-m-o-f-l-a-g-e, camouflage."

"That is incorrect," says the judge. "It is now your turn, Sophie."

"Camouflage, c-a-m-o-u-f-l-a-g-e, camouflage," I spell.

"Correct," said the judge. "Nathan, you may take a seat. You are the third-place winner."

Nathan holds his head down and makes his way to the back of the room. My main competition is gone. I really have a chance to win this entire thing!

"We are now competing for first and second place in the contest," the proctor says. "The next word for Lucy is chasm. The rock fell into the chasm."

"Chasm, c-h-a-z-m, chasm," says Lucy.

"I'm sorry, but that is incorrect," says the judge.

It is now my turn. I'm not sure if I've seen this word before, but I will try to sound it out. I notice Nathan frowning at me from the back of the room to mess me up, but I ignore him and everyone else, and think about spelling the word correctly.

C-h-a sometimes makes the cha sound, like in chair and chapter, but I think Lucy had that right. The "m" makes up the "mmm" sound at the end of the word. Lucy must have gone wrong with the "s".

"Chasm," I spell slowly. "C-h-a-s-m, chasm."

"That is correct, Sophie," says the proctor. "Congratulations, you are the winner of the fifth-grade regional spelling bee."

"Good job, Sophie," says one of the judges. "All of you did fantastic. We went 32 rounds, which is very unusual. Most of the other groups are probably finished already."

This doesn't seem real to me. Not only did I beat Nathan and the other kids, but I am also one of the first kids from my school to win first place at regionals in years.

Nathan shakes my hand and doesn't say much. I feel bad for him.

"You did a great job spelling potpourri," I say. "I don't know if I would have gotten that one right."

"Yeah, well I guess you got lucky and got a different word."

I can't believe he said that. This boy has a serious problem. I beat him fair and square. I'm through with Mr. Know-It-All.

"Congratulations," I say, heading to the door, "on winning *third* place."

Chapter 20

Queen of the Bee

I make it down the corridor and back into the auditorium. The first thing I notice is Mom's smiling face. "You did it, sweetheart!" she says, giving me a hug.

Mrs. Green comes over and pats me on the back, and other kids and parents from my school congratulate me, too. It turns out that I am the only one from Xavier to win first place. Jeffrey, Mrs. Green's son, placed second for the third grade, and two of our eighth-grade students also placed.

We wait until Mrs. McGhee gets back to the podium.

"I'd like to congratulate all the students for a job well done. Whether you placed or not, as a group you performed exceptionally, and we saw some of the longest spelling bee rounds we've had in the history of this tournament.

"In a few minutes we'll be handing out award ribbons. After that, winners in the sixth grade and up categories will compete in a spell down competition that may make them eligible for our state tournament in April. If you're a speller from the fifth grade and under, you may stay to support your friends who are in the spell down, or you are free to leave after the ribbons are passed out."

"So, that was the state bee I'd heard them talking about," I tell Mom. "I guess Mrs. Green didn't give us details because we couldn't do it until sixth grade."

I hear my name called and walk up the aisle to get my blue, first-place medal. When Mrs. McGhee places it around my neck, all the kids from my school clap and cheer. I come back to Mom.

"Let's head to the back wall so I can get a close-up shot of you with your award," she says.

We pass Nathan. I notice that his Mom, Dad and sister have joined him. None of them look too pleased.

Mom and I walk by. "Just look at that," says Mr. Jones. "I can't believe you let that girl beat you again. Instead of going to bed early in the evenings, you should have been doing more studying. Your sister never came in anything but first place. We came here from work and got your sister out of school early to see you fail."

Nathan's mother and sister look embarrassed. It seems like he is about to cry. I remember how his dad yelled at him at Fun Plex and feel sorry for Nathan. Maybe that is why he is so mean to everyone else. I decide to try to be nicer to him, even though he acts like a jerk a lot of the time.

After Mom takes my picture, I go back to take more photos with the kids from my school. Mrs. Green makes sure that I stand in the middle of the group so that my first-place medal shows front and center.

All my hard work paid off and my dreams have come true! I am the fifth-grade winner of the Houston Regional Spelling Bee! I don't have my study tiara on, but I feel like a true queen.

Dear Reader:

Thank you for reading *Sophie Washington: Queen of the Bee*. I hope you liked it. If you enjoyed the book, I'd be grateful if you post a short review on Amazon. Your feedback really makes a difference and helps others learn about my books.

I appreciate your support!

Tonya Duncan Ellis

Books by Tonya Duncan Ellis

For information on all Tonya Duncan Ellis books
about Sophie and her friends
Check out the following pages!
You'll find:

• Blurbs about the other exciting books in the
Sophie Washington series

• An excerpt from the second Sophie
Washington book, *The Snitch*

Sophie Washington: Queen of the Bee

Sign up for the spelling bee?

No way!

If there's one thing 10-year-old Texan Sophie Washington is good at, it's spelling. She's earned straight 100s on all her spelling tests to prove it. Her parents want her to compete in the Xavier Academy spelling bee, but Sophie wishes they would buzz off.

Her life in the Houston suburbs is full of adventures, and she doesn't want to slow down the action. Where else can you chase wild hogs out of your yard, ride a bucking sheep, or spy an eight-foot-long alligator during a bike ride through the neighborhood? Studying spelling words seems as fun as getting stung by a hornet, in comparison.

That's until her irritating classmate, Nathan Jones, challenges her. There's no way she can let Mr. Know-It-All win. Studying is hard when you have a pesky younger brother and a busy social calendar. Can Sophie ignore the distractions and become Queen of the Bee?

Sophie Washington: The Snitch

There's nothing worse than being a tattletale…

That's what 10-year-old Sophie Washington thinks until she runs into Lanie Mitchell, a new girl at school. Lanie pushes Sophie and her friends around at their lockers, and even takes their lunch money.

If they tell, they are scared the other kids in their class will call them snitches and won't be their friends. And when you're in the fifth grade, nothing seems worse than that.

Excitement at home keeps Sophie's mind off the trouble with Lanie.

She takes a fishing trip to the Gulf of Mexico with her parents and little brother, Cole, and discovers a mysterious creature in the attic above her room. For a while, Sophie is able to keep her parents from knowing what is going on at school. But Lanie's bullying goes too far, and a classmate gets seriously hurt. Sophie needs to make a decision. Should she stand up to the bully, or become a snitch?

Sophie Washington: Things You Didn't Know About Sophie

Oh, the tangled web we weave…

Sixth grader Sophie Washington thought she had life figured out when she was younger, but this school year, everything changed. She feels like an outsider because she's the only one in her class without a cell phone, and her crush, new kid Toby Johnson, has been calling her best friend Chloe. To fit in, Sophie changes who she is. Her plan to become popular works for a while, and she and Toby start to become friends.

In between the boy drama, Sophie takes a whirlwind class field trip to Austin, TX, where she visits the state museum, eats Tex-Mex food, and has a wild ride on a kayak. Back at home, Sophie fights off buzzards from her family's roof, dissects frogs in science class, and has fun at her little brother Cole's basketball tournament.

Things get more complicated when Sophie "borrows" a cell phone and gets caught. If her parents make her tell the truth, what will her friends think? Turns out Toby has also been hiding something, and Sophie discovers the best way to make true friends is to be yourself.

Sophie Washington: The Gamer

40 Days Without Video Games? Oh no!

Sixth-grader Sophie Washington and her friends are back with an interesting book about having fun with video games while keeping balance. It's almost Easter, and Sophie and her family get ready to start fasts for Lent with their church, where they give up doing something for 40 days that may not be good for them. Her parents urge Sophie to stop tattling so much and encourage her second-grade brother Cole to give up something he loves most, playing video games. The kids agree to the challenge, but how long can they keep it up? Soon after Lent begins, Cole starts sneaking to play his video games. Things start to get out of control when he loses a school electronic tablet he checked out without his parents' permission and comes to his sister for help. Should Sophie break her promise and tattle on him?

Sophie Washington: Hurricane

#Sophie Strong

A hurricane's coming, and eleven-year-old Sophie Washington's typical middle school life in the Houston, Texas suburbs is about to make a major change. One day she's teasing her little brother, Cole, dodging classmate Nathan Jones' wayward science lab frog and complaining about "braggamuffin" cheerleader Valentina Martinez, and the next, she and her family are fleeing for their lives to avoid dangerous flood waters. Finding a place to stay isn't easy during the disaster, and the Washington's get some surprise visitors when they finally do locate shelter. To add to the trouble, three members of the Washington family go missing during the storm, and new friends lose their home. In the middle of it all, Sophie learns to be grateful for what she has and that she is stronger than she ever imagined.

Excerpt: Sophie Washington: The Snitch

Chapter 1

My Secret

I've got a secret. Want to hear it?

Secrets are usually nice. Like when my dad surprised me with a new goldfish last year. Or the time Granny Washington unexpectedly visited us in Houston from her house in Corpus Christi.

I used to love secrets. But this one's not so great.

No one knows it, except my best friend Chloe. It's her secret, too. We don't talk about it, 'cause if we do people won't like us. And in the fifth grade being liked is as important as having a fun birthday party, or staying up as late as possible, or…Christmas.

For now, I'm not telling. Chloe's not either.

"Hey Sophie, wait up!" Chloe yells as I make my way down the hall to our first period math class. "How was your weekend?"

"The same old, same old," I reply, hoisting my math book and binder up in my arms. "Cole whined about having nothing to do, so Mom and Dad took us to the zoo and then out for ice cream.

On Sunday I caught up on all my homework after church."

Cole is my seven-year-old brother. My mom thinks he's an angel, but I think he was sent here to drive me crazy. Just this morning at breakfast, for example, he pulled my ponytail while she wasn't looking, and then started crying loudly after I whacked him with an empty Cheerios box. Of course, *I'm* the one who got in trouble. My dad is nicer to Cole than he deserves, but I think he's figured out his game a little bit better than Mom.

"Nothing much exciting happened at our house, either," says Chloe, "but I did get this cute new purse." Chloe is what you'd call a Fashionista. I admire the pretty, powder blue bag and notice the red, glittery, slide-on shoes she wears on her feet. She always manages to make our boring, private school uniforms look stylish.

"That's nice," I say.

As we near the classroom I see someone in the shadows and my heart starts to beat fast.

"Just great," I mutter.

Lanie Mitchell, the class bully, heads our way from the opposite direction.

She sees us, grins, and blocks our path. Most of our classmates are 10, like me, but Lanie is already 12 years old. She's the second tallest girl in 5B, behind Chloe, and a little bit on the chubby side.

"Hey girls, what's up?" Lanie smiles so we see her crooked front tooth and smell her sour breath.

Neither of us answers.

"Whatsamatter? You can't speak?" she snarls, moving in closer. "I know you hear me talking to you!"

"We're going to class, Lanie," says Chloe wearily, "and you're in our way."

"No, you're in *my* way," says Lanie, "and I'm not moving until you give me the five dollars you owe me."

"I don't owe you anything," Chloe retorts, hands on hips.

"If you don't pay up now, your little friend here will pay later," she says, pointing her pudgy finger at me.

Lanie joined our class two months ago. The school year has gone downhill ever since. When she first came to Xavier from another school here in Houston, most of the people in our class liked her. She was friendly and talkative, and shared the bubble gum her grandma packed in her lunch every day. But after a couple of weeks, the happy times ended.

Lanie started kicking and hitting kids who didn't do what she wanted. Since I didn't follow her orders, I became her favorite punching bag. Chloe is caught in the middle, because she's my best friend.

I'm scared to fight Lanie because I'm much smaller. Chloe is scared to fight her because she doesn't want to get in trouble. Everyone knows Chloe has a bad temper. It started after she found out she has dyslexia when we were in kindergarten. Dyslexia makes you see letters differently, so you have trouble reading. Chloe has a special tutor to help with her reading. Whenever anyone teases her about it, she fights them, so she's got a reputation with the teachers. If she is caught fighting Lanie, she might get detention, or worse.

If we tell on Lanie, we'll be called snitches, and at our school there's nothing worse than that. Two years ago, Brantley Wilson tattled on another boy who was taking his money, and the other kids *still* think of him as a snitch. They call him a baby who runs to Mommy every time something goes wrong. He barely has any friends.

Even though she is terrible to me, Chloe, and a few other kids, Lanie is nice to all our other friends. They like her. Because of that, we don't tell. Who wants to be called a snitch or tattle-tale?

Chloe reaches into her bag and pulls out a five-dollar bill. I know that is her allowance for the week.

I would offer some money myself, but Lanie has already drained my piggy bank. She snatches up the money and moves down the hall to bother someone else.

Chloe and I look at each other and quietly head into class.

I've got to make sure I stay away from that bully, I think, moving to my seat. *What's going to happen the next time I see her?*

The week has just started and we're already both broke. If Lanie asks for more money, I'm done. This is one of the worst secrets ever!

About the Author

Tonya Ellis loves reading so much that as a child she took books with her everywhere rather than put them down. She knew she wanted to become a writer after an article she wrote was published in her hometown newspaper when she was fourteen years old. Since then, Tonya has worked as a journalist and written for newspapers and magazines. She is the mom of three spelling bee champions, and has judged several spelling bee events. *Sophie Washington: Queen of the Bee* is her debut novel in a series about Sophie and her friends, which includes, *The Snitch, Things You Didn't Know About Sophie, The Gamer* and *Hurricane*. Currently, she lives Missouri City, Texas with her husband, daughter, and two sons.